This Little Tiger book belongs to:

_____

_____

_____

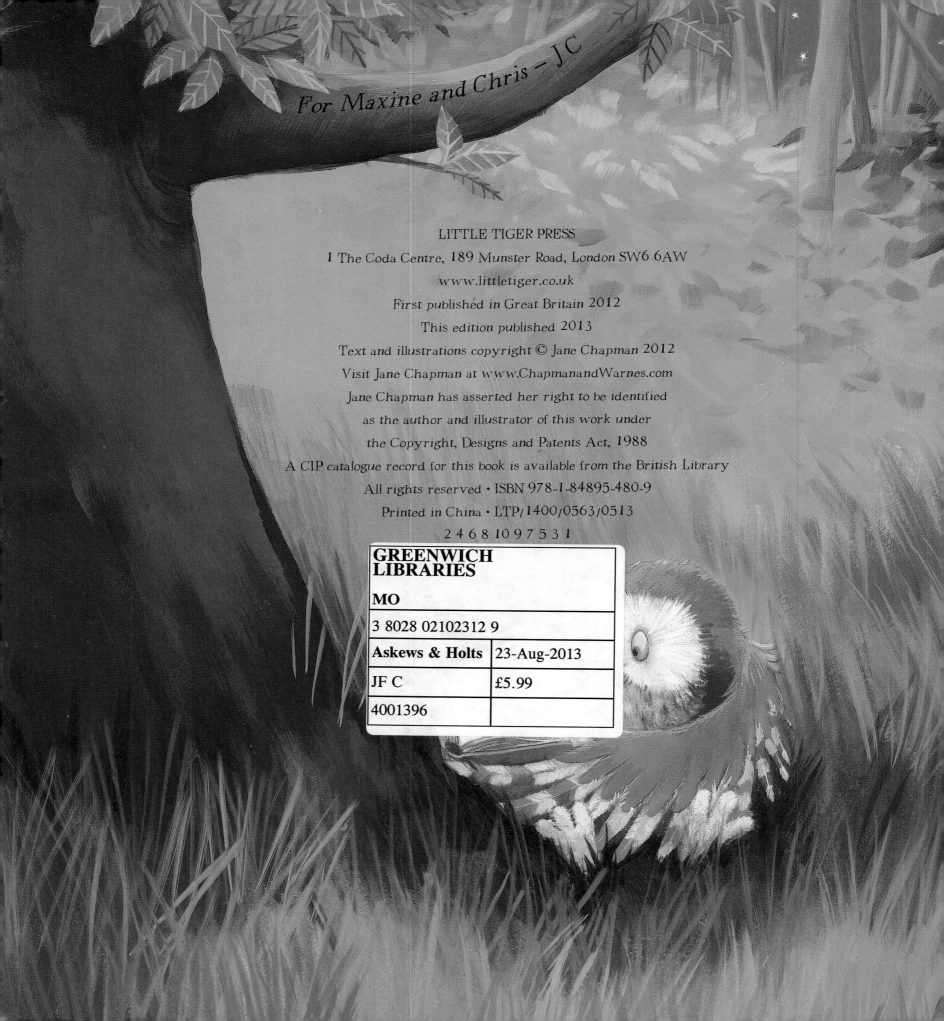

For Maxine and Chris – JC

LITTLE TIGER PRESS

1 The Coda Centre, 189 Munster Road, London SW6 6AW

www.littletiger.co.uk

First published in Great Britain 2012

This edition published 2013

Text and illustrations copyright © Jane Chapman 2012

Visit Jane Chapman at www.ChapmanandWarnes.com

Jane Chapman has asserted her right to be identified

as the author and illustrator of this work under

the Copyright, Designs and Patents Act, 1988

A CIP catalogue record for this book is available from the British Library

All rights reserved • ISBN 978-1-84895-480-9

Printed in China • LTP/1400/0563/0513

2 4 6 8 10 9 7 5 3 1

I'M NOT SLEEPY!

Jane Chapman

LITTLE TIGER PRESS
London

At bedtime, Grandma always carried Mo up to the top of the tree.

"It's a long way up for a little owlet," she puffed.

Hop...Jump...Flutter...

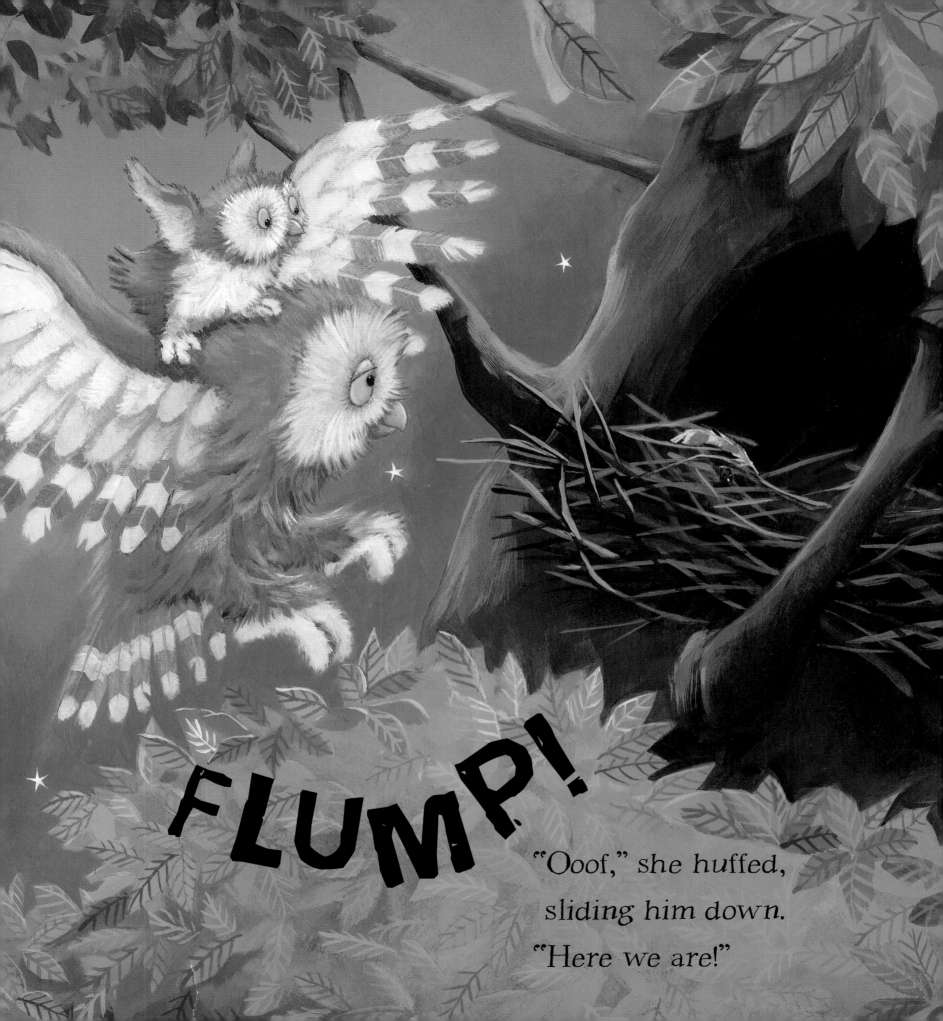

FLUMP!

"Ooof," she huffed, sliding him down. "Here we are!"

Grandma smoothed soft leaves into a cosy nest, and sat Mo carefully in the middle.

"Play with me?" giggled Mo.

"No, Sweetie, it's time for bed," smiled Grandma. And she blew him a kiss, and hopped down to her book.

The stars were fading when
Grandma heard a rustle.
"Is that you, Mo?"
"Yes! . . . And I haven't had
my Bedtime Biscuit!"

"The Bedtime Biscuit!
How could I forget?"
thought Grandma, so
she flew ...

Hop... Jump... Flutter... FLUMP!

to the top of
the tree.

Grandma sat and waited for the Bedtime Biscuit to be finished.

Mo smiled up at her.
"Play with me?" he snuffled,
between mouthfuls.
"No, Honeybun, time to go
to sleep," said Grandma.
And she blew him a kiss, and
hopped down to her book.

The last bats were going home when leaves began to rain down from above.
"Mo," Grandma called, "is everything all right?"

"No! ... And I'm not tucked in!"

"He's not tucked in!" sighed Grandma. "Up we go."

FLUMP!

Hop.... Jump.... Flutter....

...right to the top of the tree.

Grandma plumped and prodded...

and tucked and rolled ...

until Mo looked like a
wriggly, green pancake.

"Play with me?" he laughed.
"No, Pickle, it's BEDTIME," said Grandma.
"No more noise now ...unless there's an
Emergency." And she blew him a kiss, and
hopped down to her book.

Grandma sat in the stillness.
All was quiet at last. She was
just about to start reading when . . .

"GRANDMA, GRANDMA!
IT'S AN EMERGENCY!"

"IT'S AN EMERGENCY!"
thought Grandma. "Oh my goodness!"

"What is it? What's the Emergency?" puffed Grandma.

"I'm not sleepy!" said Mo.
"I don't want to go to bed.
I want to play!"

Grandma squeezed into Mo's cosy nest next to him and cuddled him. "The thing is, Mo, it's bedtime, and at bedtime SOMEONE has to go to bed," she said. "So, I have a very good idea. I'LL go to bed, and YOU can stay up!"

"YES! YES! YES!" laughed Mo,
"and you'll need fresh leaves . . . and a
Bedtime Biscuit . . . and tucking in
. . . and EVERY TIME I come up
I'll blow you a kiss."

Mo was very busy.
He didn't have time to play.
It was hard work putting
Grandma to bed.

Hop... Jump... Flutter... FLUMP!

Hop.... Jump....

Flutter...FLUMP!

FLUMP!

Hop...Jump...Flutter...FLUMP!

Most of the stars were gone when a little voice called up from below. "Grandma? ... I'm really sleepy." "Of course you are, Poppet, it's very late!" said Grandma.

And she hopped down the
tree to her favourite owlet.
"On my back," she said.

Flutter...

to his nest...

Hop...

Jump...

all the way up...

Grandma carried Mo...

FLUMP!

at the top of the tree.

Grandma snuggled Mo down
and folded soft leaves over him.
"Time for bed," she smiled.
Then Grandma smoothed Mo's
feathers gently, blew him a kiss
and hopped back down
the tree to her book.

Snuggle up in bed

with these wonderful Little Tiger books!

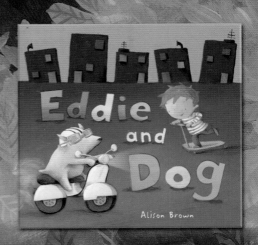

Eddie and Dog

Alison Brown

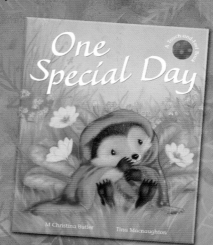

One Special Day

M Christina Butler   Tina Macnaughton

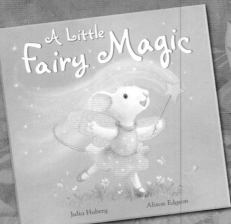

A Little Fairy Magic

Julia Hubery   Alison Edgson

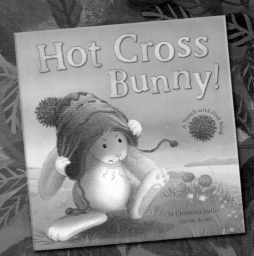

Hot Cross Bunny!

A Touch-and-Feel book

M Christina Butler
Gavin Scott

I Don't Want to go to Bed!

Julie Sykes
Tim Warnes

There's No Such Thing As MONSTERS!

Steve Smallman   Caroline Pedler

For information regarding any of the
above titles or for our catalogue, please contact us:
Little Tiger Press, 1 The Coda Centre,
189 Munster Road, London SW6 6AW
Tel: 020 7385 6333 • Fax: 020 7385 7333
E-mail: info@littletiger.co.uk • www.littletiger.co.uk